**For Miss Vernick,
redrawing the world
in her classroom
every day
—A.V.**

**For Jonathan,
who redrew my world
with the most
extraordinary colors
—H.F.**

Random House Studio
An imprint of Random House Children's Books
A division of Penguin Random House LLC
1745 Broadway, New York, NY 10019
penguinrandomhouse.com
rhcbooks.com

Text copyright © 2026 by Audrey Vernick
Jacket art and interior illustrations copyright © 2026 by Heather Fox

Penguin Random House values and supports copyright. Copyright fuels creativity, encourages diverse voices, promotes free speech, and creates a vibrant culture. Thank you for buying an authorized edition of this book and for complying with copyright laws by not reproducing, scanning, or distributing any part of it in any form without permission. You are supporting writers and allowing Penguin Random House to continue to publish books for every reader. Please note that no part of this book may be used or reproduced in any manner for the purpose of training artificial intelligence technologies or systems.

Random House Studio with colophon is a registered trademark
of Penguin Random House LLC.

Library of Congress Cataloging-in-Publication Data is available upon request.
ISBN 978-0-593-81128-3 (trade) — ISBN 978-0-593-81129-0 (lib. bdg.)
ISBN 978-0-593-81130-6 (ebook)

The text of this book is set in 18-point Garamond Premier Pro Regular.
Interior design by Paula Baver

Manufactured in China
10 9 8 7 6 5 4 3 2 1

The authorized representative in the EU for product safety and compliance is
Penguin Random House Ireland, Morrison Chambers, 32 Nassau Street,
Dublin D02 YH68, Ireland, https://eu-contact.penguin.ie.

Random House Children's Books supports the First Amendment
and celebrates the right to read.

When I Redraw the World

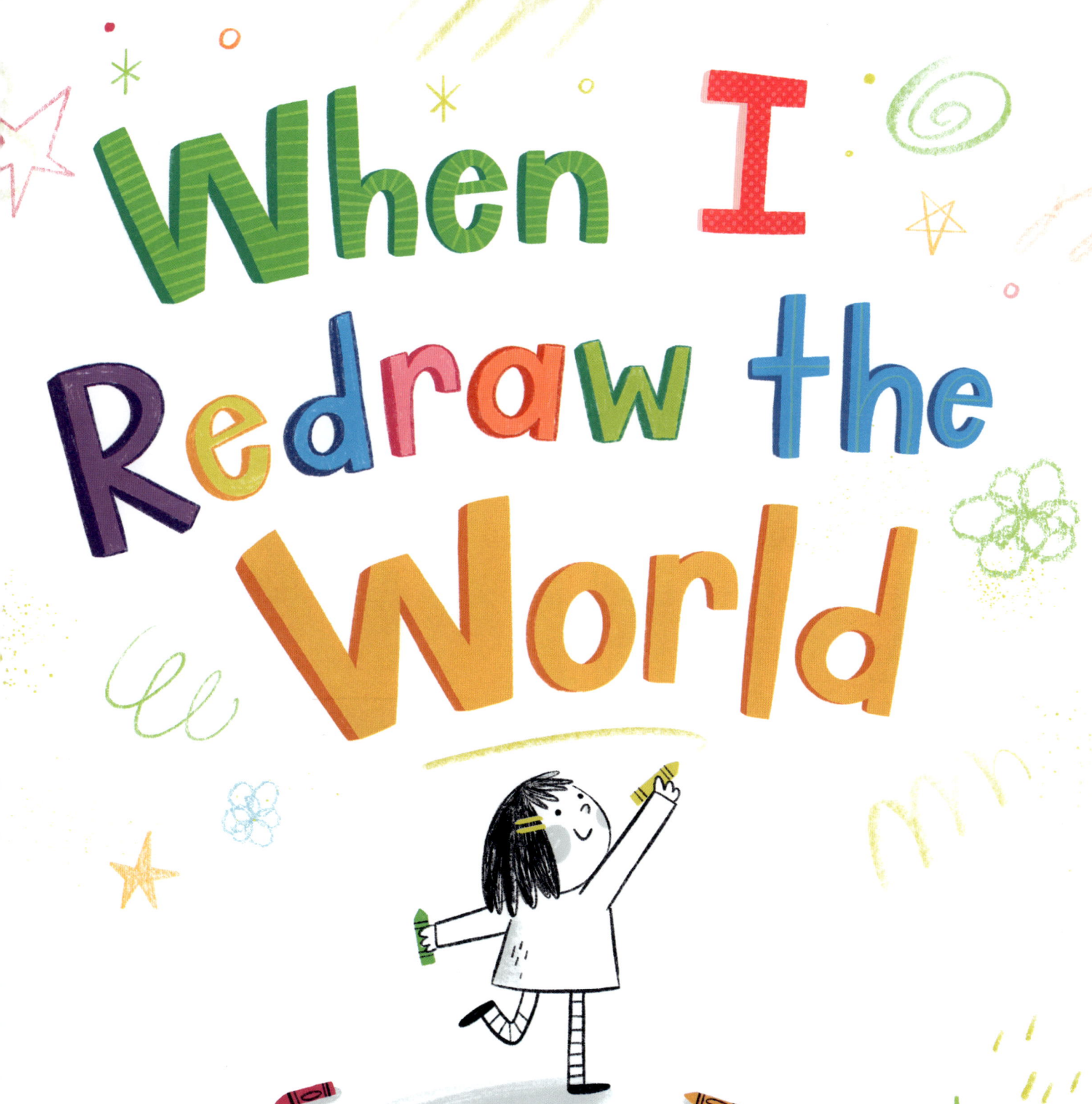

Words by
Audrey Vernick

Pictures by
Heather Fox

RANDOM HOUSE STUDIO · NEW YORK

When I redraw the world,
no one will be hungry.

And everyone will have a home.

That seems important.

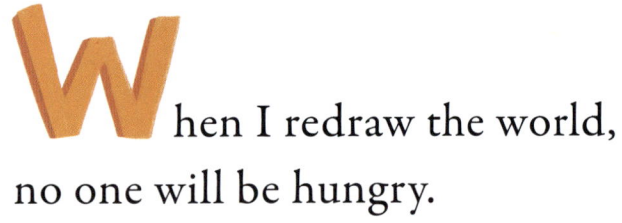

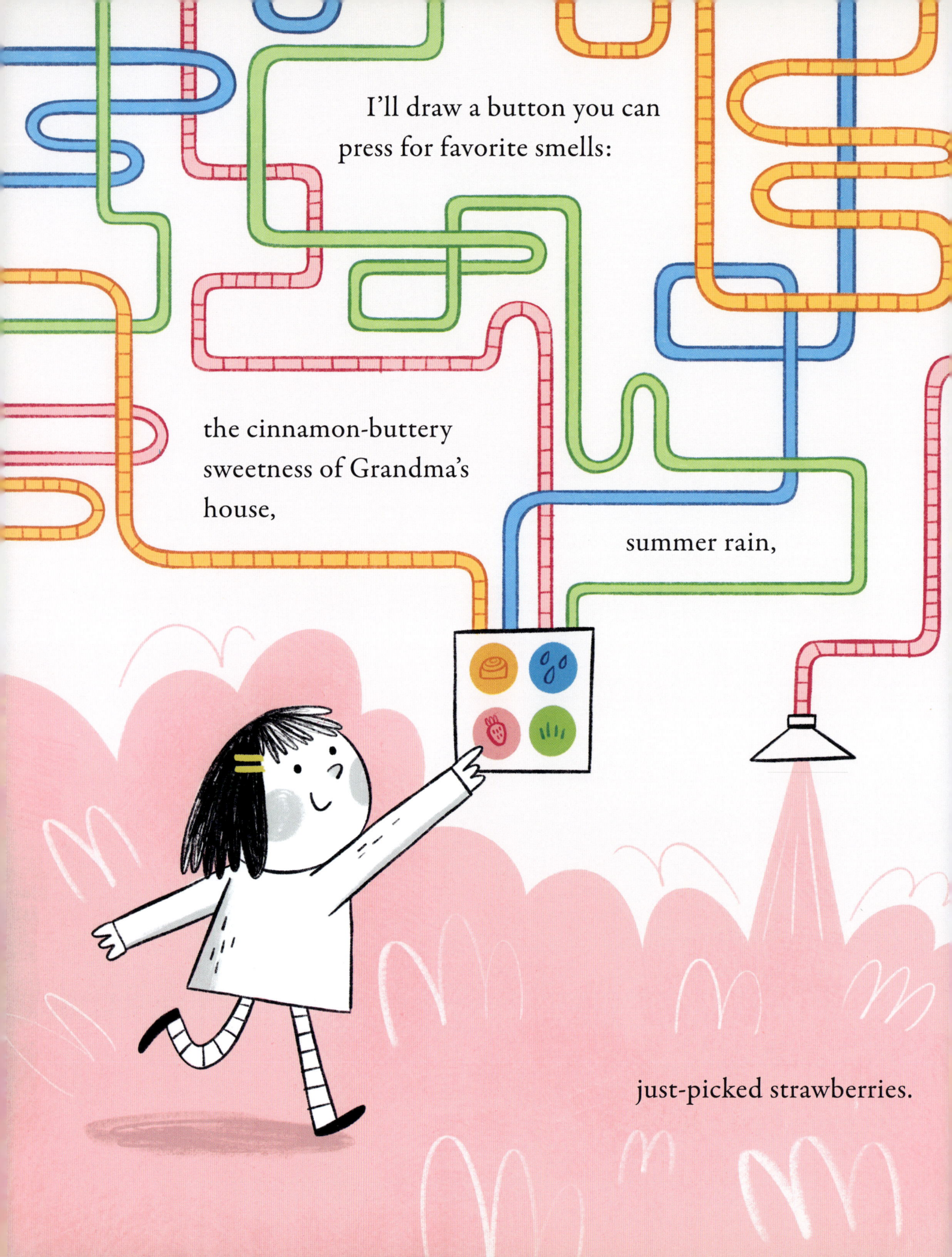

I'll draw a button you can press for favorite smells:

the cinnamon-buttery sweetness of Grandma's house,

summer rain,

just-picked strawberries.

Another button for sounds:

the sloppy lapping of a drinking puppy,

the circusy jangle of a merry-go-round.

(There won't be buttons for sights, because when I redraw the world, everything will look so amazing we won't need any buttons.)

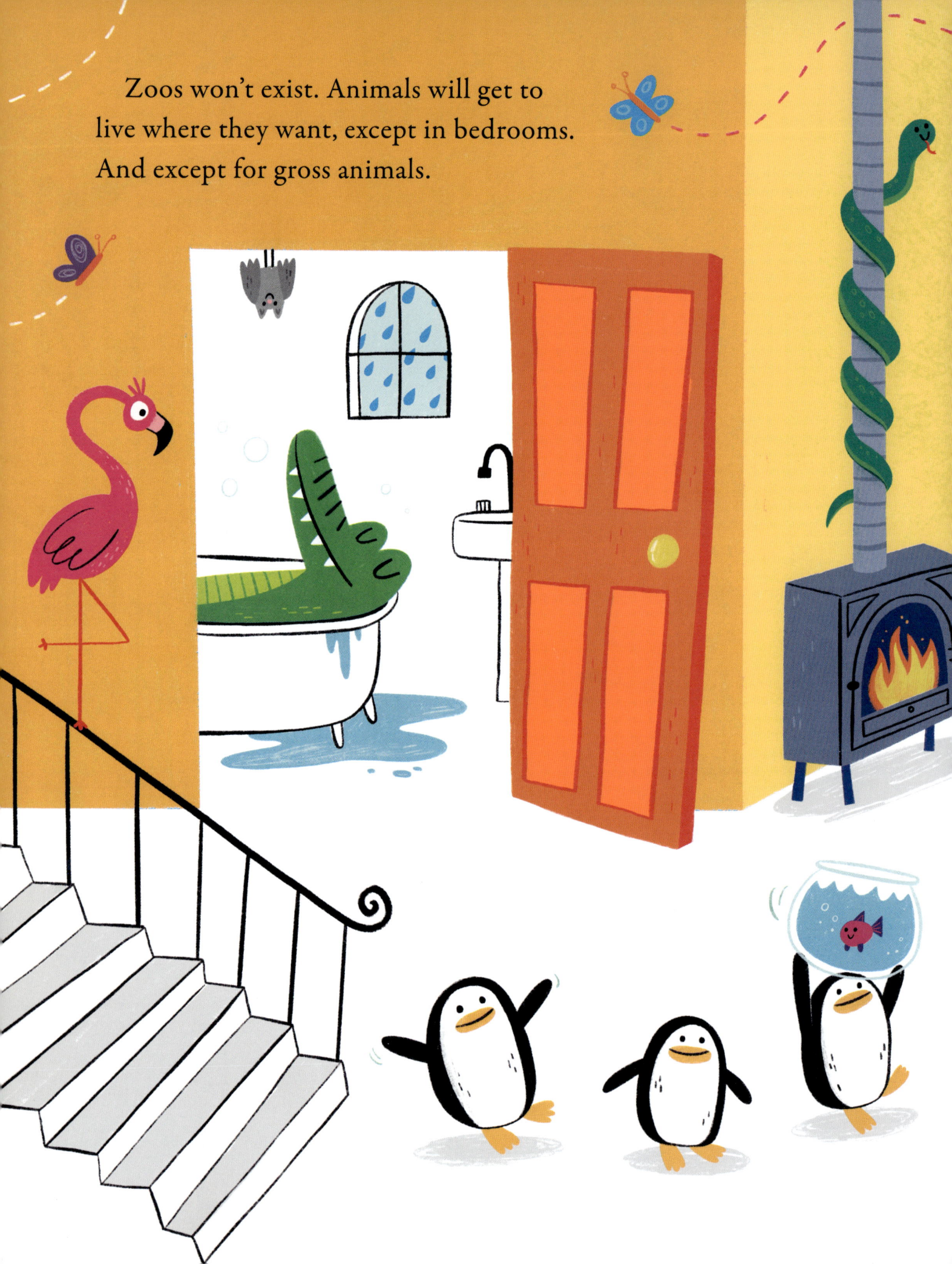

Zoos won't exist. Animals will get to live where they want, except in bedrooms. And except for gross animals.

Maybe gross animals can live together in a part of the world someone else draws. (Sorry, skeleton shrimp.)

You'll always be able to find a kind elephant, just in case you need a little help.

Lions will still chase zebras and antelopes,

but when they catch them . . .

Tea parties!

The ocean can stay the way it is—except that dangerous animals, like sharks, will have to wear costumes. Or very specific signs.

Some clouds will be close to the ground so you can feel what it's like to walk through them.

Fruit will grow at the bottom of trees so everyone can reach it.

Seasons might be optional.

Or they might change every three weeks so you get a little sunshine and a little snow but never get sick of any of it.

I almost forgot! Dogs!
When I redraw the world, I'll need to be especially good at drawing dogs because they will be *everywhere*.

Tree-house ice cream shops will be a thing. A very big thing. You'll be able to reach them by ladder or Ferris wheel.

Of course, I have to be practical. It will be impossible—obviously—to get rid of big hills and mountains. But once you climb to the top, there will always be waterslides to get you back down.

Rainbows will be the type you can walk on.

I haven't decided yet about pots of gold.

Maybe pots of hot fudge?

When I redraw the world, nature confetti—feathers, petals, stardust—will be a big thing. If someone does something really nice or generous or brilliant, confetti will flutter from trees and erupt from volcanoes.

But when a dog does something great, the confetti will be tennis balls.

"Perfect," all the dogs will think.

"You're welcome," I'll think back.

There are a LOT of decisions to make when you take on a job this big.

Maybe the world I draw should be erasable because people and animals and ideas grow and change.

But this is how I'll start.

(Just one more thing, though: When you turn the last page of a book you love, a new book—just as good or better—will appear.)